Acknowledgments

Thank you to the editors of the following magazines where these stories first appeared: *The New Hampshire College Journal*; *Tamarack Writers*; *Grue*; *The Vermont Literary Review*; *Red Eft*; *Pearl*.

Copyright © 2008 David Daniel
All rights reserved.

Published in April 2008
Publishing Genius Press
www.publishinggenius.com

Design and original artwork
by Leah Ammerman
www.cricicisdesign.com

Daniel, David
Six Off 66
Publishing Genius Press 004, 2008
ISBN 978-1-60530-548-6

Printed in Perpetua, a typeface designed by British sculptor, typeface designer, stonecutter and printmaker Eric Gill. Perpetua's high stroke contrast and bracketed serifs make it a Modern typeface with Old Style features.

for Ally

six in Six Off 66

5   THE THING IN THE ROAD

10 COLLECTING

22 OFF 66

36 INHERITANCE

42 THE MAN WHO DREAMED OF DEATH

53 THE GIRL AT THE AQUARIUM

Whoever you are: some evening take a step
Out of your house, which you know so well.
Enormous space is near. . . .
—*Rilke, from 'The Way In'*

THE THING IN THE ROAD

The trucker came upon it shortly before dawn, thirteen miles out of Ayres City, on a stretch of road that goes narrow and tricky, with state forest crowding close on both sides, and he thought he'd hit a deer. He hiked back with a flashlight.

But it wasn't a deer. "Nor like to be anything else I've seen," he told the ranger who showed up forty minutes later in response to the trucker's call on the CB. Between them they got the thing into the back of the ranger's pickup truck.

That was about 6:30 a.m.

The thing sat around the ranger's yard waiting for the state Fish and Game people to show up.

Before long, kids—who were the first to gather—had poked in one of the eyes with a stick. Later, someone who claimed to have been present would say that originally there had been three eyes and that the kids had poked out two of them; most people, however, dispute this. The remaining eye was a large, round, milky blue orb, though whether this peculiar color was caused by death or nature wasn't clear.

By midmorning a fair-sized crowd was on hand to have a look at the thing, seventy-five to a hundred people at a time, by one estimate. With the September wind lifting the vomit smell off the fresh-cut cordwood in the side yard, it was hard to tell if the thing had any smell of its own, but up close it seemed to give off a quiet musk, less tart than a bear's. "Sweetish," some said. "Nasty," said others.

Folks stood around in Pendletons and leather-top boots, talking the whole time, their voices quick and exalted and smoky in the chill air.

Shortly after 3 p.m. the men from the state finally arrived in a motor pool van. They were an unlikely pair, one too young to be that overweight. He had a small dark mustache and dimpled hands. The other, twice his age, with white papery hair and rimless glasses, appeared to be in charge. The young one looked at the thing in the yard and frowned. He had sweated through his khaki shirt just sitting and was intent on not exerting himself. The older one was full of fussy curiosity. He squatted near the thing a long time, the flesh on his neck pinched into folds by his collar and tie and tweed jacket, never mind the heat. He took notes.

"Are you the fellow who found this?" he asked someone, who said no and pointed to the trucker.

The younger, pudgy one was questioning people about where he could get some iced coffee. He was directed to the Do-C-Donut shop.

In Ayres City the thing was the only topic people talked about. All day, at the bank and at the superette and at Do-C-Donut, they talked. A good quarter to a third of them had run out to the ranger's to see for themselves.

"Some warm, huh?" the ranger lamented once the men from the state had looked the thing over.

"Yeah, late for September."

"So, what do you think it is?"

Jittery with coffee, the young man from the state mopped his brow. He for one hadn't ever seen anything like that before. But there would be no decision on the identity made here, the older man established. Nossir. There would need to be lab tests, an autopsy and biopsies, comparative analyses, tissue cultures: and those just for starters. Nossir, not today. Not by a long sight.

The trucker had stayed all day, patiently waiting to give his testimony or whatever. He felt it was his duty. After he'd talked with the men from the state, he shooed kids away from his Peterbilt and drove his load of folding armchairs on ahead to their destination.

A humorous note (though not for the fellow in question): a salesman named Ed Jubinville, from out of state, heard about it on a local AM radio talk show as he was passing on the interstate. He detoured into Ayres City, locked up his car and went to have a look. In the heat, all of his aerosol samples went up like cherry bombs, blew the windows right out of his car.

On Sunday, in a sermon, one of the ministers referred to the thing as the "Beast." Her purpose, she explained later, had been exegetical, not zoological, but the name stuck.

A teacher in the town middle school introduced the phrase "missing link" into a fifth-grade science lesson. A parent complained to the principal and wrote a letter to the newspaper, the Ayres City Advocate, railing against the school for trying to force evolution into the curriculum when it was just an unproven theory, not the truth of God.

The thing found on the wooded stretch of road thirteen miles out of Ayres City was brought to a lab at the state university, three hundred and forty miles away, and stored in a walk-in freezer, along with specimens of a gray fox and two skunks suspected of rabies, a crow that was being tested for West Nile virus, and a two-headed goat. Before the tests could be concluded, the specimen vanished.

"Chicanery in Alien Creature Case" a headline declared the next day.

The thinking was that competing scientists, eager to make names for themselves, had taken it. An anonymous phone call to a radio station's listener line said a cult of Satan worshippers had snatched it for use in rites.

A national tabloid was said to have debated running the story as its lead before going instead with "Hitler Alive in Miami Beach Nursing Home." The Ayres City Advocate carried the story on the front page for a while.

Then, other cares—municipal budget cuts, the new state-mandated standardized tests in schools, a law allowing developers to skirt some zoning restrictions, and the like—eclipsed the creature in editors' and readers' minds.

All that was some time ago. Lately another story about the disappearance has been circulating, though it is unconfirmed. According to this account, a state lab assistant responsible for carting vivisected animal carcasses to a crematorium inadvertently took the thing and it was incinerated.

The older scientist from the state Fish and Game Department, retired now, occasionally speaks of organizing an expedition into the forest north of Ayres City, but so far nothing has come of it. The City Council have talked of opening a small museum dedicated to the thing (or the Ayres City Beast or the Missing Link; there's been debate over the name) as a way of drawing tourist revenues to the once-great city. A public meeting to discuss this has been scheduled for some time next month.

A tragic note: The trucker who found the thing on the road jack-knifed his rig on a narrow stretch of Route 101 out west somewhere a few months after his find and was burned to death. Someone said he may have been high on amphetamines and liquor, leading some others to wonder if he was high early that morning outside Ayres City, too, and perhaps had invented the whole thing.

Townspeople sometimes meet over coffee at the Do-C-Donut and bring up what they remember of the day. Mostly, though, folks have moved on. The woods around there are big and dark, and life is full of pressing matters. Last Wednesday's snowstorm is the hot topic now.

COLLECTING

On the second Friday in November the ax fell, and Ed Oliver, in company with two co-workers who also had been laid off, got a little drunk before he went home to tell his wife. Kate grimaced on both accounts but took a long view: she had her part-time shifts at the bakery, thank God, and Ed was a good carpenter; there'd be other jobs. By Thanksgiving, however, new housing starts in the Merrimack Valley had dropped to zero, and one day at lunch Kate said didn't Ed think he should go down and sign up to collect? He looked at her. "Well, it takes time," she said. "They don't just hand out checks." Then, like his staring was ignorance and not something else, she added, "There's a waiting period."

"I'll find something," he said and went back to eating.

They had the same discussion a week later, and his answer was the same, though his tone of voice may have been different. He did one small job, hauling an old freezer in his pickup, and made forty dollars. Kate said the unemployment office had computers where he could check job listings, at least show he was looking while he waited for his claim to be processed.

"What claim?" he asked.

Still, twice that week he drove past the employment assistance office downtown, the tires of his six-year-old Dodge Ram buzzing on the cobblestone street. Reflection on the office windows made it hard to see what was going on inside, but he thought the place looked busy. On the day of his second drive-by, he went to the Forge.

The Forge was another kind of office for the unemployed. If there were some work available that Ed could do, he figured he would hear about it there. Half the patrons seemed to be out of jobs, and Kenny Robillard, the owner and bartender, was a counselor of sorts, roving among the bottles and softball trophies on the backbar, dispensing consolation and drinks. "Wives and bosses are like a dirty diaper," he told Ed one time, Ed forcing a smile and saying he knew the punch line; but Kenny gave it anyway and Ed felt small for having used Kate as an opener. After that he didn't bring up the tension at home, he just asked if anyone knew of any jobs. Didn't matter what, he said; sheetrock, finish, whatever anybody had. Roofing.

On mornings after he dropped his two daughters at school, he sometimes drove around thinking, twitching the radio dial, bits of music and talk coming at him the way it used to when the bedside radio would awaken him at five a.m. and he would snuggle warm a moment against Kate's back before rising in the dark to dress. Those were boom days, when there had been a lot of developers building condos and what were called executive homes, half-a-million-dollar units on two-acre lots scratched out of hilly woods in Tyngsboro and Groton. Ed loved those days, never grudging the people who had the kind of money to buy such homes. His joy came from making a project take form, quit being lines on blue paper and start to fill space. It was a joy he took home with him at night.

He drove out there one morning in late November. Only the oak trees still had leaves, brown clusters that rattled in the wind, holding on. Many of the houses stood unsold, realtors' signs pegged hopefully in eroded lawns. Some remained unfinished, turning a dim gray as the particleboard weathered, scraps of Tyvek flapping like semaphores. Once the big tech firms had started to lay off, it was simple arithmetic: no executives, no executive homes. Builders went belly-up. Ed drove home feeling frustrated.

At supper one evening, Kristen, six, said that her friend was going to Disney World over the holiday vacation. Jenny, eight, sneered, "That's for little kids. I'd rather go to Apricot Center, wouldn't you, Dad?" Ed caught Kate's look and changed the subject. Later, as he lay awake on his side of the bed, Kate asked from hers what he was thinking about.

"Florida?" She sounded surprised. "The girls don't really care about that. They understand."

But it hadn't been Disney World that Ed was thinking of. He was thinking about his own father, who had been a lineman for Light and Power. One time during a long strike, his father, union-bound but unable to see his family suffer, had elected small-scale disaster instead. They were living on the South Shore of Boston at the time, and on a blazing July day his father and his father's friend slogged out on the mudflats and dug clams with a garden spade, wearing sneakers instead of boots, no gloves, damn near breaking their backs. Then, carting four bushels—four hours' work—in the family car, they set up along a busy stretch of 3-A with a hand-lettered sign and waited for the money to come rolling in.

After several sunburnt hours, the only person who stopped was a state warden, badged and wearing a sidearm. Did they know the penalty for clamming without a permit? For selling unchlorinated shellfish? They were looking at fines, maybe jail. Ed's father dumped the clams, not having made a nickel. For weeks after, the car carried the smell. Eventually the strike ended. Much later his father retired, taken care of by the union he'd served for forty years. His folks lived in Maine now, having gone north, while everyone else, it seemed, went to Florida.

That's what Ed had been thinking of, and thinking that if he had to put in forty years, starting now, he'd be seventy-seven when he retired. He couldn't imagine being seventy-seven.

* * *

Tired of the Forge, Ed sometimes went to other bars. On Pearl Harbor Day a guy in one of the bars was complaining to a waitress about the Japanese and how we'd been covering their ass all this time and what were they busy doing but shafting us. The guy had a small gold ring in his ear. "They're smart, the Japs," he was saying, "gotta give 'em that. They live like sardines and save their money. Take one bath, all in a big tub." The waitress said it was cultural. "I know it's cultural," the guy said, "I'm just saying. I'm giving a for instance."

As Ed drank his beer he noticed how his hands no longer had calluses. They weren't the hands he had always had. Someone could have cut the hands off a bank teller and sewn them onto his wrists for all he could tell the difference. The guy with the ring in his ear, who couldn't have been any more than Ed's age, and therefore not even born until the mid-1950s, was insisting how Roosevelt was the last true leader the country had had.

When Ed got outside it was quiet, and he stood on the sidewalk getting his bearings. This wasn't a neighborhood he came to often. A soft buzzing filled the mild dark. It was the neon beer signs in the windows, but he pretended the buzzing was his brain working.

He started for his truck. If there was a bad winter, and if he sprang a grand for a plow, maybe he could make some money plowing snow. Sure, along with five hundred other guys who already had plows. He wondered how the economy was going to change when nobody in power seemed to want it to. In a way he almost hoped it wouldn't change, as if then he would be justified in the anger he was beginning to feel. During the Depression the country had set up programs to help people get back on their feet. Still, some folks had chosen to drop out; they hopped freight trains and just took off. He thought about what that would be like, drive away from here and keep going.

As he reached his truck, he saw a car stop down the block and kill its lights. Someone emerged from a building and went to the driver's window. Ed realized it was the second vehicle he had seen stop there in all of three minutes. Like the other, this one drove away almost at once. When Ed drove past the spot a few minutes later he noticed a guy standing up against the front of the dark building.

There was no planning. Ed went around the block and parked. He walked back. Maybe it was the booze, or the mild air for December; he felt calm and purposeful. Down the block he could make out the guy still standing in the shadows, smoking a cigarette.

Ed approached, walking slowly, but not too slowly. He glanced at the guy—short, with bushy hair—and looked away. That was his sole instant of hesitation. He lowered his shoulder and plowed the guy hard into the building. The cigarette flew from the guy's mouth and hit the wall in a spurt of sparks. In the next instant, both of them were on the sidewalk. Ed grabbed the man's throat in one hand, pinning his head. The guy struggled. Ed shoved his free hand into a coat pocket. Empty. Tried another pocket, yanking the lining out. With it came several small envelopes, like sugar packets. The guy was shouting words Ed didn't know.

Ed squeezed harder, afraid now, not sure where he wanted to take this. He ran his hand over the guy's clothing. The guy brought a leg up, trying to hook Ed off. Ed shoved the leg down and felt something on the guy's ankle. He pulled it loose. One of those elastic ear bands skiers wore, dark with white letters. Inside, rolled in a tight wad, was money. Ed got up and ran.

His heart was still thudding when he parked in front of his apartment, a city mile away. He tried to slow it with deep breaths. The white letters on the ski band, he saw now, said Mt. Snow. He removed the money and spread it out. What had he expected? Fifty, sixty bucks? There was a lot more.

With his bank teller's hands he started to count. At every car that passed, he stopped, moving only his eyes to check the mirrors. When he finished counting he looked up at the darkened second-floor apartment, then back at the bills in his lap. God, there was seven hundred and eighty-two dollars.

He waited two days before he showed Kate six hundred of what he'd taken. It was under-the-table money, he lied, for a counter he had built. Kate was glad for it; happy for him. Eventually she got around to asking if it was work he could count on. He said he didn't know, he doubted it. It was a good buffer though, he said.

They were standing in the kitchen, she washing dishes while he re-wired the toaster. They never used the dishwasher anymore. Jenny was doing math problems at the kitchen table. Kate gave her a problem involving how long six hundred dollars would last a family of four if they spent so much per week.

"Don't start," Ed told her.

"Who's starting? The money's great, but it's gone like that." Wet from the sink, Kate's fingers made only a damp snap. "We need steady money, and you're entitled."

"Kate."

"It isn't charity. They already took it in taxes. You paid for it. I don't know how to make it any simpler than that."

"I don't either, dammit. I'm not going on the dole."

Maybe the saucer slipped. It hit the floor and broke in a spangle of white chips. Jenny looked startled, and Ed was just able to hold his temper. Glad that he'd kept his own buffer out of the $782, he put away his tools and went out.

At the Forge, Kenny Robillard said he had news. UPS was going to be putting on a couple of people to wash trucks for the busy season. He had talked to someone he knew and had mentioned Ed's name. Ed should come by next day at three and Kenny would introduce them.

At nine a.m. he dropped Kate at the bakery, then went up to Nashua and spent most of his buffer money on a Christmas tree and gifts. As he paid a cashier at Child World, he wondered how many hands the bills had gone through. Would anyone care that the money had once paid for dope? He doubted it. If people bore prejudice against a dollar's past, everyone would walk around with empty pockets. He put five bucks into a Salvation Army kettle.

Back home he hid the gifts and set the tree on the porch. He shaved so close that when he splashed on Old Spice his skin stung. He put on a blue shirt and a tie with little golfers on it. The tie had been a gift once from Kate's parents, though neither they nor Ed had ever played golf. An idea came to him and he telephoned Kate at work and told her not to take her break until he got there.

"What's wrong?" she wanted to know. "Is it one of the girls?" He laughed and said just wait, okay?

He arrived wearing his maroon blazer and smiled at the surprise on his wife's face. They went through the drive-up at Wendy's and got sandwiches and coffee, then parked. She told him again how nice he looked. He apologized for last night. She reported a discussion some customers were having earlier, a nice old man saying it was too cold to snow, and a woman saying, "Too cold? You think Antarctica's warm? They got snow a mile deep there." Kate said she hadn't spoken up but she kind of knew what the old man meant.

They drank coffee out of paper cups with holly designs on them, and Ed promised to set up the tree that night so the girls could decorate it. Kate said she'd make popcorn. When she had to go back to work, she straightened his tie. "Good luck. I have a good feeling about this." As she scooted toward the bakery door, he thought her denim jacket looked thin against the cold.

The Forge was quiet. Kenny Robillard told him he smelled like a French whore. They went in back where cartons of empty Bud longnecks formed an aisle to Kenny's desk. Kenny jutted his chin at the phone. "I just got off. Sit down."

That's when Ed began to have a bad feeling. He took a chair that faced the desk.

"It's not even Phil's fault—Phil's the guy I was telling you about, Phil Castro—it's somebody up in Human Resources." Ed knew Kenny was telling it just the way he had heard it; he wouldn't say Human Resources. "They hired a couple college kids to wash the trucks."

Ed sat a moment without speaking, then he said, "Yeah, well, college costs money." He undid the tie and took it off and folded it into the pocket of the blazer. "Thanks for trying."

Kenny said, "Shit. Let me buy you a drink."

It was dark when Ed got outside. The wind swirled straw in the nativity display outside city hall. He wished he had worn a real jacket. In a liquor store he spent the last of his money on a pint of Fleischmann's. The streets were thick with evening traffic and he drove around for a while, not thinking about a plan; then he got on Route 93. Moving against the flow of cars, he headed for Boston.

In forty minutes he was downtown. He parked on Tremont Street and opened the pint of whisky and took some of it down in small swallows. Capping the bottle, he slipped it into his pocket and got out and locked the truck. He walked toward Park Street. There, near the subway stairs, he entered the Common.

There were carolers out, and families braving the cold to look at the Christmas displays. It was colder now, with the wind funneled by the buildings, shaking the bare trees, making lights on them tinkle and dance. He chose a path at random, moving deeper into the Common, away from the lights, slowing to nip at the bottle. Through the trees he could see the frog pond, drained now, a scar in the darkness. He walked past it, seeming to recall that the city used to let it freeze for skaters, but not sure.

On the far rim of the Common was a baseball diamond. He made out the glow of cigarettes and a group of figures standing near the backstop, hunched against the cold. He toked the bottle once more, then capped it and set it on a bench, still half full. As an afterthought he took the necktie from his pocket and wound it around the bottle and left that, too.

When a man appeared from the trees and said, "Drugs?" Ed kept walking. On Boylston Street he exited and made his way back to his truck. He opened the lock-box in the bed and got out a framing hammer. He pushed the head into the pocket of the blazer and started back to the park.

It was late now, nearly ten according to the clock on Park Street Church. Most of the sightseers had gone home, leaving only the street people, who clustered near the T entrance where the subway exhaled warmth. He stayed on the paths, moving again toward the frog pond. He passed the same way as before, aware of the dark lines of sticks and dead leaves collected at the edges of the empty concrete basin. He touched the heft of the hammer in his pocket. He was heading beyond the pond when a voice said, "Wanna get high?"

Ed kept moving. "Hey, man, I axed you a question." The figure drew closer, and Ed saw he was a youth, tall, wearing a long leather coat and a wool cap.

Ed drew the hammer from his pocket, the heavy straight-clawed head snagging for an instant, then pulling free. He turned. "No, I want your money."

"Shit." The kid bolted, plunging into the darkness of the trees. Ed hesitated, then went after him. They were running hard, zigzagging between tree trunks, the youth's long coat flapping. Ed was close, and when the kid swerved to avoid a bench, Ed took him down.

They hit the frozen ground together and began to scuffle. Ed rolled him over and, using both hands, pressed the shaft of the hammer hard against his throat. The youth stilled, both of them breathing hard.

"What you want, man?"

"Your money, jewelry," Ed said, knowing there'd be gold around the youth's throat. The youth cursed and started to struggle again. In the dark distance, toward the baseball diamond, there were voices. The youth shouted. Ed pressed harder with the hammer. "Shut up."

The youth kept shouting. The other voices were closer now. Ed raised the hammer above his head, anger suddenly fully upon him. And now the youth fell silent. They looked at each other, and in the youth's eyes Ed recognized fear. Suddenly Ed pushed to his feet. Without a word, he turned and walked away.

He drove back to Lowell, physically unable to go faster than fifty-five, not letting himself think what might have happened, but unable finally to void the idea of people following him home. In the dark of the apartment, when he let himself in, the balsam fragrance came to him like an accusation. Avoiding the front room where the tree would be, he went into the bedroom his daughters shared. The walls were night-lit by the nativity display the girls had set up, with plaster animals and one of their dolls, out of scale, as the baby. Standing there, listening to his children's breathing, he began to tremble. Afraid that he would wake them, he went into the front room.

The tree stood in a corner, decorated, a sheet spread palely beneath it like a drift of new snow. For a long time he stood there in the darkness and shook, feeling that his life was over.

When he went into the bedroom and began to undress, Kate stirred and mumbled, "What time is it?"

Late, he told her. He said he had to get up early. She turned to face him. "It fell through," he said. I'm all balled up, nearly killed a kid, could've killed myself, he wanted to say, but he said, "I'll be getting up early. I want to be downtown when the office opens."

Kate pushed up on an elbow. A lick of hair lay dark across her forehead. She asked no question, but it was there in her waiting.

"It's time," he said.

"Do you want to talk about it?" Her voice was rusty with sleep.

"No. Get some rest. Tomorrow."

"You sure? I never want you to do something you don't feel okay about. We can always . . ."

"No. It's time."

After a moment she lay back down. He used the bathroom and got ready for bed, then he lay down and drew up the covers. "We can talk in the morning," Kate said. "I'll make a big breakfast."

After a few minutes, softly, because the silence demanded it, he began to talk.

For some reason he was talking about the summer his father had dug the clams and tried to sell them and ended up having to dump them. The warden, maybe acquainted with discouragement and failure, or just sympathetic to fellow working people, had let them go. Remembering, Ed spoke of how, as a boy, he had felt his father's defeat. Not that his father would ever have spoken of it, any more than he would have voiced the pride with which, several years earlier, after a long week of hurricane overtime, he had brought home a crisp one-hundred-dollar bill in his pay, looking on as his sons each handled it, more money than they had ever touched before. Ed told this, and other things that came to him (of Christmas snows, and huddling before the baseboard heating vents on cold mornings with his brother Jake . . .), not sure why except that he found in the telling some comfort.

Kate's murmurs had become the gradual sigh of sleeping, but he didn't mind. He drew closer, near enough to feel wisps of her hair fanned upon the pillow and to breathe her scent, balsam, he recognized now, and the fainter smell of the bakery, and he was warm there where he lay on his side, the wool blankets fisted to his chin, the world dark and snow-silent as he went on talking in the dreaming house.

OFF 66

OGDEN, NEW MEXICO
POP. 241

The sign slipped past, and George Lowrey found himself startled at how small the place was. (How small was it? Tired one-liners flitted through his mind. Both city limits signs are on the same post. The preacher can reach from the pulpit to wind the clock at the back of the church.) But Lowrey felt no humor, only a slow-feeding anger that had been growing like the dust settling over the sea-blue sheen of the Benz since he had left the highway a dozen miles back.

Or perhaps the anger had begun two thousand miles ago, in Manhattan. He had envisioned himself riding into town to the cheers of simple townsfolk as an avenging gunman of old, or the commander of a liberating army. But, in fact, as he angle parked by the raised sidewalk, the only welcomers were a raucous crow perched on a sagging roof before him and a dog that barked feebly a couple of times before settling down to gnaw its tail.

As Lowrey climbed out of his car, the noon sun was so sharp even his Ray-Bans did not blunt it completely, and he had to peer under his palm, surveying the weathered façades of the small businesses that flanked Ogden's main street. It damn sure wasn't West 57th.

He pressed the small of his back and stretched. He had made a more or less straight haul from New York. The car had run perfectly—as it damn well ought to, the money he'd paid for it. But what the hell, it was only money, and the way his new paintings had moved, money worries were history. Funny thing, money. When he was sleeping on a floor in SoHo he used to think a few hundred bucks a week would do him. Later, when he'd begun to sell some canvases it was give me thirty grand a year, that's all I need. Now? There were still critics like the putz who claimed Lowrey's work lacked "humility," but the public was buying. His accountant said he was going to have to go into limited real estate partnerships and muni bonds soon or become a big patron of the IRS. Lowrey didn't know what he was making, but it was a lot—a whole lot—and that felt good.

Even better, though, was the feeling he got when he painted: an almost magical sense of making something appear, cityscapes arising brightly as if out of thin air, his imagination made manifest. It was at such times that it seemed as though the canvas could not handle the fecundity of his vision, the mad flourishes of his brush, the big primary color splashes of his palette, the canvases themselves growing bigger and bigger, till now some could cover an entire loft wall.

Thinking of his work relaxed him somehow. When the tension in his back eased, he pulled on his silk sport jacket and picked the nearest store, eager just to get in out of the glare. The sign read: Gates' Hardware. A pimply teen in engineer-stripe overalls bobbed behind a glassed display chest of hand tools. No doubt he'd been peering out to see what had caused the gala greeting party. He gripped his pants straps and came over, looking eager. "Help you, sir?"

Lowrey resisted a comment about who really needed help. "I'm trying to get a lead on a man who once lived in Ogden. His name was Fred Lowrey."

The eager look held out for a minute before sagging to something akin to idiocy. "Gosh, beats me," the kid said. "My family bought this store a year ago, so we're kinda new."

Lowrey was amazed. Who would make a choice to come here to stay? The only conceivable attraction would be watching someone paint you into the population number on the sign outside town, and that thrill would wear off fast.

"Is there someone around who isn't new?" he asked with deliberate patience.

There was, and the kid told him where he could find her. At the end of the street Lowrey went into the Moon Café. Camilla Reyes, the middle-aged owner, came from a family that had been around "since the conquistadors," if the wit at the hardware store could be believed. From behind the counter the woman gauged Lowrey speculatively. "Not a Witness are you?" she asked.

He narrowed eyes not yet adjusted to the dimness. "What?"

"'Cause if you are, we got no truck. I believe in live and let live, and my living is this place. So if you got objections, or the Watchtower to pass out, kindly take 'em elsewheres."

Lowrey slid onto a stool, noticing for the first time that the place was a saloon. His anger was on a back burner now, cooled slightly by the locals he'd encountered so far, but the low flame of purpose didn't flicker. As he asked his question he opened his billfold and withdrew one of the dozen hundred-dollar bills inside. There was also a five-hundred-dollar bill, which he'd asked the teller at the Chase for on a whim.

"Give me a Stoli martini, and buy everybody else . . . "

Peering around he saw that the extent of the crowd was a single long-haired old man. "Get him one, and whatever you're drinking."

The woman frowned at the bill then at him. "Martini."

She fixed it and set it before him with the change and brought a draft beer to the old man in the corner, who raised it to Lowrey in thanks. When the woman had settled herself behind the bar with a glass of wine, she said, "Lowrey, huh? You missed him by forty years."

"You've got the wrong man," he objected.

"Nope. Fred. He took off when he was young and joined the service. He never came back here that I know of. The last of the Lowreys kicked off, or left these parts back in the '50s. There was one, Bill Lowrey, used to work on the railroad, but he's long gone."

Her facts seemed right. The navy figured; and there had been an Uncle Bill. Listening to the brief genealogy, Lowrey felt his purpose fizzling, escaping like air from a punctured tire. Somehow the car outside, the designer clothes, even the nicely padded wallet, lost meaning. He slid a ten off the pile of change on the bar. "Again."

He tried to pry more information out of Camilla Reyes, but she was scarcely more communicative than the dog in front of Gates' Hardware. The Lowreys had been quiet folk who kept to themselves; yes, it was the navy; no, she had no idea if Fred Lowrey was dead or alive.

He sipped a third martini, perversely enjoying the spike it was driving into his head. There wasn't even a gravestone around for the Lowreys, nothing he could so much as go by and spit on. Instead, he reckoned bitterly, he was going to have to content himself with the highway to Santa Fe and preparing for the show. But as much as the exhibit would mean for his career, this little turd of a town somehow stood like a barricade to his satisfaction in the show and his career and even in painting. Crazy.

It took him a moment to grow aware that someone was standing at his elbow. Squinting at the face in the backbar mirror, he saw it was the old longhair from the corner table. An Indian. Probably hoping for more firewater. Lowrey ignored him. His sense of having been cheated in Ogden, New Mexico was too keen. He went back to his drink.

"I heard you asking about Fred Lowrey," said the man quietly.

Lowrey turned to regard him directly. "What?"

Lank, graying hair framed a face that looked like a brown paper bag that had been crumpled, then partly unfolded. The tattered serape the man wore over faded work clothes slipped a little on his gaunt shoulders. "I knew him."

Lowrey gauged him a moment. "You want a refill?"

Lowrey suggested they go to a table. He got his change and left a tip. As he stood up, he lurched and realized the booze on an empty stomach had hit him pretty good. But when he had walked across the room and sat again, he was in control. "You knew the son of a bitch, huh? When'd you see him last?"

Despite Lowrey's tone, the Indian was calm. "A few years ago."

"And?"

"And what?"

"C'mon, c'mon," Lowrey said irritably. "What do you know?"

"Did you know him?"

Lowrey blinked, taken aback. Did he know Fred Lowrey? God. Hadn't the man haunted the first twenty years of his life? And become something like an obsession in the past year? He leaned closer. "He had a wife he married at the end of the war. They had an infant son, and one day when things were tough,

Fred Lowrey decided he didn't like responsibility, so he took a hike. A long hike. He never came back. I'm his son. Now what was he like?"

The Indian studied his own worn hands, one side then the other. Finally he looked up. "He was an SOB who ran off and left his mother and brother and sisters to join the navy after Pearl Harbor. Sounds like he did the same with his own family after the war. I haven't seen him in several years." He swallowed the rest of his beer.

Lowrey stared at him, left again with his anger and nowhere to put it. "You said you knew him. How? Did you grow up in this bustling metropolis, too?"

The Indian had settled into himself, as patient as weeds, and Lowrey wondered if the man really had known his father at all. Maybe he was just a booze mooch. But what the hell, he wasn't scoring points any other way. "You want another?"

When the beer came, the Indian said he had met Fred Lowrey long after Fred had left Ogden, after he'd left his wife and son even. There wasn't much to tell. The old family place was still outside town. Lowrey's mood rose only slightly above the lethargy of disappointment and the alcohol. "Show me," he said.

* * *

The road wound for a few dusty miles, forking several times, at which points the Indian would motion a direction with his hand. Otherwise he sat silent, apparently unimpressed with the air-conditioned ride of the Benz. After a while he said, "Here."

Lowrey drew off onto dirt alongside rusted railroad tracks and stopped. Beyond a cluster of rocks and cottonwoods was a crumbling structure. Over the years he had pictured the house in his mind, but always as something different. What he saw now was little more than an adobe shell, abandoned to the desert sun and wind.

"That's where Fred was born," the Indian said. "He lived there with his mother and brother and sisters till he . . . well, like you said, till he took a hike."

Lowrey felt victimized all over again, the way he had as a child when his mother explained why he didn't have a father like other kids, how his father had had some problems and left. But in spite of that, goddammit, George Lowrey had made it. He was a good painter, and with time maybe he'd become a great painter. His canvases were bought before he painted them. And next week his work would hang at an exhibit in Santa Fe alongside New York paintings by Georgia O'Keefe and Edward Hopper. And yet he still felt cheated by the man who had lived in that old ruin, robbed even of revenge, stripped of his hope for some sort of liberation.

The Indian was watching him. "Want to have a look?"

"Screw it." Lowrey was suddenly eager to be gone.

"You sure?"

"Hey, what is it with you? You too proud to be selling blankets and tomahawks out on the highway, you've got to peddle bullshit information and worthless tours?"

The deep-set eyes in the dark, seamed face were on his. Feeling awkward all at once, Lowrey reached for his billfold. "Forget it. Hey, bet you can't tell me whose picture is on a five hundred dollar bill."

The Indian turned away. Lowrey took out the bill. "McKinley. Here."

Ignoring the money, the Indian opened the car door and got out. "Keep it." He closed the door.

Lowrey stared at him in disbelief. Stuffing the bill away, he motored the window down. Instantly a wave of hot air hit him. If he stayed out here in the middle of nowhere much longer he'd be as wacky as the Indian. "Get in, I'll drop you back in town."

"I can get where I'm goin' from here."

All at once the thought of being here by himself made Lowrey nervous. "You must be roasting in that blanket. Come on."

The old man seemed to read his mind. "Need directions back to the interstate?"

Lowrey cursed. He yanked the car around in a gravel-slinging turn and gunned off. And only gradually did the air conditioning begin to cool the heat of his fury.

As he racked up miles, heading west on old Route 66, he began to get beyond his feelings enough to wonder: Had the Indian been keeping something to himself? Hinting at something unsaid? Knowledge that Lowrey, caught up in his bitterness, had missed? The thought began to cultivate a whole crop of doubts. Resisting them, he ground down on the accelerator and watched the speedometer climb.

But he hadn't gone five miles before he slowed the car, made a U-turn, and started back to Ogden.

* * *

The last daylight had been siphoned from the sky by the time he parked on the main street. The Moon Café was busy now. Couples in boots and western wear two-stepped to songs on the jukebox. At the bar the woman was gone, replaced by a man in a vest. Lowrey asked about the Indian, but the barman hadn't seen him.

It took time and several wrong turns, but he found the road they had been on that afternoon. At last he made out the pile of rocks and drew off the road by the rusted tracks.

The desert had made its change, and he shivered as he closed the car door. But it wasn't only the dropping temperature, he realized: he was a little afraid. Beyond the cottonwoods, ghostly now in dark, sat the crumbling adobe house. Inside something brushed the walls with orange light. Turning up the collar of his jacket, he approached. "Hello?"

No response. Somewhere not far off, an animal yowled. Coyote? Outside of movies, he'd never heard one.

Through a window opening he saw the slide of reflected light, and then he heard a crackle of flames. Edging nearer, he peered inside—and jumped!

The Indian was seated on the floor by a campfire. Lowrey had the impression that the man was staring straight at him, and yet he hadn't moved. Fighting off his disquiet, Lowrey said, "It's me. George Lowrey again."

Now the Indian moved, motioning with his hand. Lowrey picked his way around to an opening and went inside. Part of the roof was missing, and overhead the first stars shone. The back half of the structure was covered, and in the dancing light Lowrey saw a table, cupboards, some pots and pans. There were clothes hanging on nails and several rolled tarps in a corner. Along one wall lay
a pallet bed. He turned back to the fire and the Indian.

"Is this really where Fred Lowrey lived?"

The old man looked up, shadows crawling through the ravines of his face like snakes, and Lowrey wondered if having come back was a mistake, if maybe he'd been better off tackling the lines on the Rand-McNally atlas. But, no; he couldn't go on being jerked back and forth by his emotions. He had to lay his questions to rest and get on with life. "Was it?" he pressed.

After a silence, the Indian said, "What do you know about your father?"

Lowrey didn't hesitate. "That he was a cheap, selfish asshole." The words spilled out of a cauldron, acid-tasting on his tongue.

"Opinions," the Indian said quietly. "Give me facts."

"He left a good woman and an infant son and took off."

"Truth."

"He left a G.I. allotment and sent small checks at irregular intervals—but he never once wrote so much as a word."

Again the Indian confirmed it. If Lowrey had expected more, however, nothing came. Seized with anger, he grabbed the old man by his serape. The cloth tore as he yanked him to his feet. "Goddammit, you talk, or I'm gonna—"

Lowrey stopped, his voice dribbling away. The dark eyes had seen violent emotions before; they weren't shocked by them any longer. Lowrey let go and stepped back. The Indian straightened his serape, barely noting the rip in the cloth. He remained standing. In a low voice he said, "Today I agreed with your opinion of Fred Lowrey because you already knew what you wanted to hear. You came full of anger—you're still angry. There's part truth in what you say, but you miss the whole truth."

"Then tell me!"

Taking his time, the Indian wandered into a corner, picked up something and tossed it. A woolen blanket. "Sit."

Checking his impatience, sensing it was the only way he would get anything from the man, Lowrey squatted. He tucked part of the blanket under him as a cushion for the dirt floor and flapped the rest over his legs. His clothes were useless against the growing desert cold. The Indian came back, firelight and shadow shifting on his face. Lowrey watched him pull the serape over his head, lay it aside, and open his shirt.

"I spent my first twenty years on a reservation. When the war came I joined up." Through the open shirt, Lowrey made out a faded swirl of ink. The man pulled the shirt open wider. Now patterns seemed to swarm over his lean torso: a star, a bucking bronco, a firebird, other designs he couldn't make out.

"I got the first of these in San Diego. The old story—stewed, screwed and tattooed. Except for that one time, every other line on this body was a sober choice. You know, I saw the South Pacific—Midway, Guadalcanal . . . I saw men die, and other men in planes with little circles painted on the wings kill themselves on purpose. But it was back on the reservation, after the war, that I got my real shock. I'd already known I didn't fit in elsewhere, but I sure didn't fit into that little government corral either. So I left. Drifted. I worked oilrigs in Texas and Oklahoma, shrimp boats on the Gulf. Up in Montana I hired on horse ranches. And places I'd go I'd pick up some ink, like these people with the Winnebago campers collect stickers."

Listening to the monologue, aimless as it seemed, a tale of wandering, Lowrey saw the skin of the Indian's face and body slowly becoming a roadmap of his life. And hearing it, George grew restless too. The story seemed to have lost direction, drifting as randomly as the man had during those years. "Was it in the navy you met my father?" he broke in, wanting to know.

"No, that came later."

"Where?"

The Indian was silent a moment. "You're a painter, huh?"

Lowrey tried to remember if he had said it; he was pretty sure he hadn't. The man retreated to a corner and brought back a roll that Lowrey took to be another rug. Squatting near the fire, the man carefully unrolled it. In the orange flicker, Lowrey saw it was a painting, done on oilcloth: a mustached man swallowing a sword. On a second panel an obese woman in a tiara and tutu stood tiptoe on pixie feet; a wolf snarled on a third.

"What do you think of them, Painter?"

Lowrey frowned. They were crudely done, anatomically inaccurate, but painted as they were, on shiny cloth, in vivid color, they had a definite visual impact. "Did you do them?"

"Your father did."

Lowrey wondered if he was being put on, but the Indian was looking at the paintings. Lowrey bent closer. And all of a sudden he was very afraid. He drew a steadying breath. "You said before there were different amounts of truth . . ."

"You know your father ran off, left you and your mother. Do you also know about the disease he picked up in the South Pacific?"

Lowrey felt his fear closing in. "No." He croaked the word.

"A tropical disease. Like jungle rot, which plenty of guys got in their feet. It's a fungus gets between the toes and starts to ooze and itch. Then the sores dry out, the skin cracks, and you think it's cured, till it begins all over again. A lot of guys still have it forty years later. Well, your father got something like it—but his didn't stay down on his feet. It started to creep up his legs. He went to a doctor back there in Boston."

Lowrey listened. Doctor, singular, became doctors, intrigued by this malady they had never seen outside of obscure textbook references. They prescribed powders and salves, to no effect. In fact, the disease worsened, moving up Fred Lowrey's torso, leaving a trail of wet sores and a maddening itch. Out of desperation someone suggested a treatment that was still brand new and unproven. The Indian didn't know the name, but from his description Lowrey guessed it was radiation therapy.

"Trouble was it was expensive. More than your father could ever afford. But his problems weren't only money. Greased all over with ointment, he wasn't very appealing. He knew your ma wanted a big family, and she was patient with him, but he could see her torment, see the hidden revulsion cross her face whenever . . . Well. He finally decided to handle the situation another way. So, yeah, we're back to your half-truth. He left. He didn't tell her because he knew she'd try to stop him. Yet maybe deep down inside she wouldn't want to. Think about that."

Lowrey couldn't speak. The Indian went on. "He came back here to the desert, figuring to get his own treatment. And eventually it worked. The sun dried him out."

"He . . . he was here the whole time?" Lowrey asked. "My mother said the checks he sent were sporadic, never from the same place twice."

"A man does what work he can."

Lowrey fingered the oilcloth portraits of the sword swallower, the fat ballerina. "He was a sign painter?"

"That was just the one time so far as I know."

"Then, I don't . . ."

The Indian rose and from the corner brought another oilcloth roll. "Like I said, the desert dried up his disease. But afterwards his skin was all ridges and welts. This picture here . . . " He unfurled it in the firelight. It was a fanciful painting of a man whose bare torso was crinkled like the tread of a snow tire. "For sixteen years in a carnival sideshow, your father was the Crocodile Man."

* * *

George Lowrey wasn't sure how long he sat. Cold had settled into legs long gone numb. Gradually his shock went to pity, then finally to a painful sense of having been wrong. The Indian concluded briefly. "I knew your father from the sideshow. I was called the Human Roadmap. He told me about this town with the warm sun and peaceful folks. This was his house. He willed it to me."

"So he is dead," Lowrey said.

"Five years now. But he knew about you, and your painting. He told me. He was proud. And till the day he died, your father was the best, most generous friend I ever had. He'd lived a lot of years alone, with people seeing him as a freak, but he always said, 'you look at a person, it don't matter spit what his outside's like'."

Although a part of him wanted to be gone, Lowrey did not move immediately. Again he offered money, but the Indian shook his head.

"Sell me something then. These paintings."

"They're yours by right. You're his son."

Which was true; but Lowrey knew he could not take the paintings. They belonged here. "I'm paying for your company, then. The sunset earlier, hearing a coyote."

Done resisting, the Indian shrugged and bent to tend the fire. Knowing a check would never get cashed, and the picture of William McKinley might be too much trouble, Lowrey put six one-hundred-dollar bills on the blanket. He drove across the star-washed desert to the highway, then down the straight ribbon of 66 toward Santa Fe.

INHERITANCE

You squint through the opening and see your family: father, mother, brothers (both younger than you). Smiling. Behind them the fountains of St. Louis sparkle prismatically in the June sun. You take the picture.

    It's easily the twentieth snapshot you've taken in the past three days as the train has brought all of you from Boston, the blue and white cars of the Spirit of St. Louis winding southward, giving you your first look at these places where a small piece of your heritage lies, giving you gently rocking nights in the Pullman, stopovers and soda and "samishes," (as the old black porters call out as they stroll through the cars), and the sluggish coffee-brown curl of the river. You studied the Mississippi this year in geography and are already storing away details to carry back to the eighth grade.

    In an hour you'll board the Lone Star Limited going south to Texarkana, then on into your mother's home state, where you will take more pictures with this new camera that your father bought which gives back the black-and-white images in only two minutes. A "land" camera, he calls it, though you're not sure why; you've taken pictures of people and water and they've come out good. Wet even, though only for a little while.

"Let's see it, sis!" Jason demands.

"No, me!" cries William.

But you keep the snapshot against your blouse, resisting their smudging little-boy fingers. You hand it to your father. "Nice," he says, barely looking. "Your turn." He takes the camera and motions for you to pose, but you won't. You want to take pictures, not be in them. "For your boyfriends back home," he teases.

Your mother comes to your defense, remembering perhaps being thirteen, though you doubt it. She seems stranded always in adulthood, abstracted with details you cannot imagine being busy with.

"She's at that age." Your brothers pick up her words.

"At that age."

The mimicry carries them sporting to the big stone pools full of bronze mermen and copper fish, where water scallops and splashes and breaks into chips of the rainbow, exciting you.

Across the busy square a big sign has drawn your father's interest. You look at the foreign words: ANHEUSER BUSCH. "There's a brewery nearby," he says. "Smell it? Hops. They give free tours." You ask for the camera back and he gives it up, his mind already elsewhere. ("But be damned careful, that thing cost me an arm and a leg.")

"Then how can you walk, Dad?" Jason laughs.

"Yeah, you'd be Hops-along Cassidy," says Tim.

Taking their hands, your father sets off. You don't want to go, you tell your mother. You're content here in the busy square, in the sun. You want to take pictures. You've had this discussion before, your mother and you. She casts you that look, long and wistful, then, hesitating, trails after the others. She hesitates again, caught between, and then calls one caution: be here so you can all board the train together. You're sad just a little for your mother; but then, left alone, you're joyous.

You gaze around, feeling your parents' former days in this city before you were born. Your father, a short man in a dirt-brown uniform, assigned to the Army Engineers. (You used to think he drove trains, and only later learned he worked on the river somehow.) Your mother, photos tell, in a broad-shouldered dress and a smooth, purled hairdo, smiling past the spill of hair: a pretty, slender girl barely six years older than you are now and already a wife. And before they left this temporary city you were conceived. That's the word; you've seen it in books in the library, the "i" before "e" exception. Conceived. You say it to yourself again.

That's when you decide to see something of this place where all that happened.

Your family members have vanished into the pigeon-and-people swarmed sidewalks. You wait, then cross the broad plaza and begin to walk. Slowly, as you wander, you create out of remembered old photographs and family tales those days before you were conceived. But now, in 1958, oddly, you know something else that you are sure your mother never told you of: a great loneliness. Hers.

Yes, you definitely feel it here and try to match it to the smiling young woman in the snapshots, her hair in a style like an actress named Veronica Lake. Your father hadn't permitted her to work, so she hadn't cut her hair short like other women, who had jobs in factories.

You stop walking, rocking back slightly as if this awareness were a tall wave passing against you, through you. Then you move on, compelled now by some tidal drift, a current that grows, bringing you with it. A little afraid, but unresisting, you go.

And you take pictures, sighting through the small window on the camera back. Signs, buildings, the joinings of streets, which make no sense. Once, you stop walking and snap a picture of a place on a corner, with a neon sign that says simply "Lounge"; later, you take two shots of a second-floor office window with gold lettering, which you cannot read in the gleam of the sun. Nor do you wait to examine the photos that emerge; you merely slide them, still sticky (like newborn babies you imagine), into your white patent leather purse.

Again you experience your mother, thirteen years back in this city, and it is 1945 as the War draws to an end. You feel her aloneness, abandonment almost, like a child left behind at a railway station.

Then . . . yes, you feel that too. Friendship.

A man.

He stands in line behind her at a department store and talks to her. He knows what will make her laugh. He . . . understands. Tall, dark, with curly hair. Yes. They go for coffee. He walks her to her bus. They meet. Coffee again; then drinks. Not once. Often.

And the war ending. Your dad out of his dirt-brown uniform, taking his bride north in a car they don't make anymore, shiny black as your purse is white, home toward his family, away from her Texas. The loneliness ebbs. In their lives, other life flows. Suddenly you are aware of now. You've got to rush. They'll be worried, your dad angry, brothers gleeful at the crisis. You retrace your steps, experimentally at first, then with sureness, moving with swift, almost inborn knowledge in this place where you have never lived.

Yes, there is the foreign sign and the fountains, glimmering horsetails of water, rainbows that vanish. You run into the cavern of Union Station and see the Lone Star Limited. You hurry, the camera jouncing against your chest. They see you, your brothers crying out, scattering pigeons as they run stamping to meet you, flapping souvenir pennants. CARDINALS. You dad, beer-smelling, his voice booming so that other passengers turn, but relieved as he rounds up your brothers and hustles them toward a stack of portable steps where a wrinkled brown man is looking at a large watch in the pink palm of his hand. You offer your dad the snapshots you have taken. He is crowing to your mother that he knew you were fine ("She gets her sense of direction from me!") and scarcely looks at the photographs, only at the new camera, checking that it is safe and that you are, too. Then the men of the family are up the three steps into the train.

It's your mother who fingers the snapshots in the narrow passageway of the railroad car, looks through the printed streets at the black and white buildings, the park, the place with the neon sign ("Lounge").

"Why?" she asks, her look uncertain.

Why did you take these pictures, she means. You don't know and you say so.

She turns, looking past you, then glances at the two shots of the shop with the name in gold on the second-floor window, about to hand them back to you—and stops.

One snapshot is a blur, you see now. In the second, the delicate filigreed letters are legible.

"Aaawwwlll aboarrrd," bawls the conductor's voice.

But your mother has not moved from the passageway. She is staring at the photograph, her lips shaping soundless words. And you, tall for thirteen, can see the snapshot, can make out the writing on the shop window. RICARDO BLOUNT * PSYCHIC READER.

That word, "psychic"—like "land" camera . . . you aren't sure of it. But you don't ask because you see your mother reach for the wall of the slowly moving train, a look of shock on her face as she starts to sag as if under some terrific burden of memory.

THE MAN WHO DREAMED OF DEATH

There were Smitty, Petras, Bolduc, Bonetti, the others, good guys to have in your squad because they were bright and eager and wary. I didn't know any more about soldiering than they did, maybe less, and I told them this, but perhaps to an 18-year-old, someone 22, with a couple years of college, seemed wise. They stuck close, asking their questions, running their endless riffs about home and the war, the girlfriends they might marry first chance they got, how that first beer after boot camp was going to taste. Sometimes I liked to get off alone to try to digest all the training coming down so heavily. Hotly too; it had been in the muggy mid-90s most of that July at Parris Island, South Carolina.

It was several weeks into the cycle, and we were doing pugils. Pugils are these big sticks, padded on both ends, which you use to try to beat your opponent's head to jelly inside a football helmet. The DI had called a break, and we were waiting for noon chow. I was sitting in the meager shade of a pine tree trying to ignore the biting flies. Bravo squad lounged nearby. Spread around the grove, T-shirts stitched with ribbons of drying sweat, sat the whole company. Across the clearing the training cadre smoked and talked. I was hoping they were debating giving us the afternoon off.

I glanced up without interest as Joe Kord came over. I knew Kord casually as the leader of Delta squad. His guys, some of whom, like him, planned to be officers, were critical of him I'd heard, so he had become a tyrant. We had avoided the problem in Bravo. We were New Englanders mostly, and to a man, none of us had any intention of doing one single thing more than we were told. It was 1968, and we had become Marines by the worst of all means. At the Army base in Boston, a recruiter had come in and said he needed men to fill a quota. No one volunteered, so he picked. Smitty, Petras, Bolduc, Bonetti, me.

Not Joe Kord though. He had joined up down South someplace, Georgia. Now he stood there, sweating and wearing a reddening welt on his throat where a pugil stick had got below his headgear. He said to me, "How you like it so far?"

"Sticks?"

"That, weapons, hand to hand, all of it. You like being a jarhead?"

"Shit."

Kord thrust his hands in his pockets; then, maybe remembering that this was forbidden, he pulled them out. "Hey," he said in a soft voice, dropping into a squat, "did you ever moon over the air rifles on the back of comic books when you were a kid?'

I squinted at him. He was a lanky kid, his head too big for its thin neck. I said, "Daisies, yeah, but I never got one."

"You're getting one now. We all are."

My faint grin was all the invitation Kord needed. With a quick look around, he hitched closer, "I mean, we're going to that war, man. Like it or not, we're there."

I considered this a moment, but said nothing. It was too hot. But Kord was not to be deterred. "Glenn" (outside of Bravo, Kord was the only guy who used my first name), "do you believe in fate?"

I raised my eyebrows, so odd-sounding was the question; but his face was earnest. "Not sure, I said, "Do you?"

With no hesitation he said, "Absolutely."

He was one of those guys who are quiet until they know you, then a floodgate is raised and it all comes. Your interest or lack thereof is incidental. I remember one evening a week of so after that, when Joe Kord and I were getting along okay. He came into the barracks while I was writing a letter. He had a paperback book of stories he had got at the PX that he thought was uproarious, told me I ought to read it sometime it was so funny. There was one in there he had just finished, about a guy who finds himself on dates with four different women in one night, none of them aware of the others. "Listen," Kord said and sat on my bunk and began reading aloud. I wanted to finish the letter; I didn't write many, but I tried to make the ones I did write worth the read. Still, from time to time I listened to his story, maybe to be polite. On he read, never looking up. When he finished, I found nothing even remotely funny about the story. It was a dull masturbatory farce for lonely soldiers. Hearing it depressed me. When Kord left, I put my unfinished letter away and tried to sleep.

But that was later. That Tuesday, though, as we sat there on the sand waiting for the chow truck, Joe Kord started talking about a dream he'd had.

"It's in a forest. I'm walking along when, all of a sudden, in slow motion, I feel myself . . . no, I see myself getting iced. Shot in the back of the head, jerking in this kind of dance-y way, then tumbling down onto a trail. I see leaves swirling up slowly, splattered wet and red. My head's got this clean hole in it. Here." He twisted and touched the button on the back of his skull, which shone through his GI haircut. "I've had the dream maybe five times since boot camp started. It's mostly always the same." He looked at me intently; then, with a swift glance over his shoulder, his voice sinking to a whisper, he said, "I know what death looks like."

It had a corny sound, a TV sound, yet I found myself troubled, and I knew why. It was his sense of certainty. He regarded the dream as a glimpse of some coming reality. He was convinced it would take place just as he'd dreamed it. As evidence of some kind, he cited a dream that he said had come true, some minor thing that proved nothing. Squinting past him, I saw the chow truck lumbering up the sandy road. Around us, other boots started rising, moving into the clearing. Kord said, "It'll be Vietnam, Glenn. I'm positive. Everything fits. The jungle, the trail. I'm a lieutenant, and I'm shot to death."

"In a dream," I said.

He shook his head. "It's too real." He leaned back and let his breath out. The welt on his neck seemed to throb hotly. His fatalism, the heat, my weariness irked me.

"Look, if you're so sure it'll happen, don't become an officer." I started to get up, but Kord's hand on my arm held me.

"I have to. I've got to face it."

Come on, I thought, why me! I gazed helplessly after the others already falling in on the mess line. Chow was one of the few routines I welcomed.

"There's something else," Kord went on. "Something that bugs the hell out of me. In the dream I get this feeling that I'm killed on account of . . . an oversight. Some carelessness by somebody else."

There was no option open but to grin. "Sounds like what the DI's been telling us got through your steel pot into your wooden skull."

His head moved back and forth on its thin neck. "I mean it. I'm not a careless person, but I'm going to die."

I shooed a fly and got up then and joined the others.

* * *

Perhaps having in common that each of us was older than our fellow trainees, Joe Kord and I built a small friendship. We talked when we had time. He could be engaging in a boyish, Southern way. In me, who knew? Maybe he saw someone who made at least a pretense of listening to him. Plus, I had been drafted after a few years of college in Boston; perhaps he, too, mistakenly credited me with wisdom.

At rushed meals in the mess hall, on bivouac, at night as we polished boots and brass, we sometimes talked: sports, a bit about women, little about ourselves. Sometimes the topic of his dream would find pretext to come up, usually at his mention, and he would put it on me, retelling it, each time adding to the myth of his own inexorable acceptance of fate. With the passing weeks, I understood why Kord's squad had tired of him (though not because of the dream; I was pretty sure I was the only one he had told). He tried too hard, hogging a relationship with his nervous energy, as if afraid of judgments which might follow if he let down. This, plus his roundabout prying into my sexual experiences, finally cooled me toward Joe Kord.

By then, however, we were nearing the end of the training cycle. Days were running at a high pitch, and for once there seemed to be no time for pettiness to intrude. In the final week we took tests. The mental tests (first aid, military protocol, the UCMJ) were written, so no one knew where he stood overall. The physical tests though were carried out head to head, and a lot a psyche went into them. Of the squads in our company, my Bravo and Kord's Delta were on top. The rivalry was heightened by the North-South face-off. Delta, most of whom bragged they'd been squirrel hunting since they could walk, won handily in the weapons round, but we edged them in PT. At the end, we finished dead even. To the cheers of the full company, Kord and I shook hands.

When we got our orders, five guys from Bravo, including me, got combat assignments and were ordered for further training. Joe Kord got his guaranteed officer school and was scheduled for leave before reporting to Quantico. For a few uncertain moments I wondered why I hadn't given thought to going that route myself; then I remembered why, and I never thought about it again.

On our last evening as boots, everyone got together for goodbyes. Kord came out to the ball field where Bravo had played a reckless game of football until it had grown too dark and were now drinking beer for the first time in eight weeks. I was sitting against a tree with a quart of Black Label when Kord came up. Without a word, he handed me something, which I saw was a sealed envelope. Squinting at it in the dusk, I saw my name printed on it.

"New orders," I said, "right? Telling me this was all a bad dream. I can go home."

He seemed uncomfortable. Soldiers were clustered close by, drinking beer and talking. "Can you come with me a minute?"

"Where?"

"Just for a minute."

I pushed up and followed him unsteadily away from the group. "What's going on?"

"That's the dream. I wrote it out this afternoon."

"Dream . . ."

"About how I'm going to die."

"Oh, that."

"It's all there, dated and signed."

"C'mon, have another beer. We'll drink to long life, and all the—"

"Keep it," Kord cut me off. "Open it sometime when you're sober."

I stared at his face, trying to read it. More quietly, he said, "I've got your home address. I'll write your folks and get your military address. When I arrive in-country I'll give your address to someone, so he can write you and describe how it was."

"Shut up, Kord," I said.

"What?"

"You know what the hell you're talking about? I'm the one's gonna be humping the boonies. You'll wind up drilling poor boots like us at some stateside camp. The war could be over by the time you pull a commission."

His pained frown said he was disappointed in his choice of confidant, but it was too late to find another.

On a clean system, a little alcohol goes a long way. I'd drunk a lot, and my mind was frayed out; I couldn't hone a proper edge of anger. Eight weeks of hell were over. Truth is, I felt good. I gripped his arm. "Listen, that's not the point, man. It's a dream. Look, if you're so sure about this, why not cop out? Don't go OCS. I mean, be just a grunt like Smitty and me and Bolduc."

He swore and made a snatch at the envelope in my hand, and I should have let him take it. But all at once my haze of good cheer evaporated. I rammed the palm of my hand against his chest. He stumbled awkwardly but kept his feet. I shoved him again. "Are you crazy?" I said. "Why get shot for nothing? You want to die?"

I stopped. For the first time I found myself doing what I had resisted since that hot noon under the pines when he had first told me the dream: I was arguing with him in the terms of his fantasy, as if I too were convinced it would happen. Angry with him, with myself, I started back to the ball field.

He came with me. "I have to accept it. Just go along, will you? I'm not trying to be a pain . . . it's just there's no one else I can tell. Promise you'll keep the letter. Will you, Glenn?"

I turned. My frustration didn't ease. I struggled to build a solid and damning argument to topple his fatalism once and for all. Nothing came. The ring of laughter from across the field, and the sounds of insects and tree frogs, wove us into the fabric of the late summer evening. I took the letter. He shook my hand, and with surprising mildness he said, "Go home and get the women."

After boot camp we were all scattered. I went to Lejune. In the training regiment there I found only one soldier from my original company, a black guy from Charlie squad I hadn't known. It was my first bitter taste of military friendship: intense, loyal, doomed. Smitty, Petras, Bolduc, Bonetti, the others—I never saw them again; and after a while I seldom thought of them. I forgot Joe Kord too.

* * *

There was an incredibly schizoid sensation being in the bush. The green-on-green paddies and jungles, swaying gently one moment, bristling with gunfire the next. Kids slopping happily in mud puddles, smiling and calling you, "Number One GI"—or turning and fleeing, like you were the Reaper himself. I stayed angry most of the time: with the fuckheads in power who had put me there, with what I perceived at home to be a conspiracy of uncaring, at the pussies who had beat the draft, with everyone and everything except the men I was with. And this became my shield and armor. I was a good soldier. I listened up and I learned and I didn't make the same mistake twice. Things I had sneered at in training became my credos.

I did ten months with the 1st Division, most of it up near the DMZ. Then, in a single engagement, I got wounded twice; fittingly, once by us, once by them. A corpsman with a New Jersey accent and bloodstained whites said, "You'll make it, soldier. Give us five minutes."

I got back to the world with eight months to do, and they sent me to Pendleton. It was there, in California, recuperating, that I began to sense what was happening. The whole country was feeling pressures as great as any brought on by a massive firefight. I got a letter from a college friend living in Canada; in it, he told me that a mutual friend had killed himself with heroin.

It was also at Pendleton that I met Joe Kord again.

I had a light-duty profile and was undergoing physical therapy. Shopping in the PX one day, I saw him. He had 2nd lieutenant's bars. With him, pushing the shopping cart while he filled it with groceries, was a slight, brown-haired girl. I went over.

"Joe Kord," I said. "What's happening?"

He was a little slower making the connection, surprised no doubt at seeing a gaunt enlisted man with a cane, addressing him by name. I understood; a year can be eternity. At last it seemed to dawn on him, but he checked my nametape to be sure. Perhaps I imagined it, but he seemed to pale a little. "Glenn Oliver. Hey, how are you, troop?"

We shook hands, and he introduced me to his wife, Cathy. He told her to take the cart through checkout, that he would meet her at the car.

"Jeez," he said, clapping my shoulder tentatively, as if he might knock me over. "I want to hear what you've been up to. Can I buy you coffee?"

We took stools at the snack counter on one side of the PX, and I gave him the nickel tour, leaving out a lot of it. He, on the other hand, grew talkative and began to tell pretty much everything he had done since boot camp, up to and including his current post as a supply officer. He had met Cathy back east on a pass five months ago, and they had married when he got assigned out here. He had never been closer to the war than this. He said he was considering staying in for a chance to make rank. I said I was looking forward to getting the hell out. After a while the coffee was gone; he poked the button on his watch. "Hey, I've got to dee dee mau," he said, using the Vietnamese phrase. "Cath'll be waiting. You married yet?"

I said I wasn't.

"Still the old playboy, huh?" His laugh had an explosive, empty ring. I never had been a playboy, but I recalled his constant prying questions in boot camp.

Conversation had dried up, and I sensed him growing nervous for some reason, eager to be gone. I should have let it go, but curiosity, piqued by his briskness, made me ask.

"Letter?" His puzzlement was not genuine, but I played along.

"In boot camp. About a recurring dream you'd had?"

"Oh, God." Again the hearty, hollow laugh. "That. That was . . . wow. I'd split up with a girl. Back in Atlanta. It's a closed chapter now, but at the time, man, I thought I really loved her. That dream must've been the old Foreign Legion thing." He tried a grin. "You don't still have it, do you?" He cleared his throat. "The letter."

"It got lost."

He seemed relieved. "What's done is done, right?" He stood and I did, too. "Hey, good seeing you, Glenn. I hope things turn out for you."

"You, too."

There was no talk by either of us about getting together. For a moment, Kord hesitated, and I imagined I saw something rising toward the surface of his thin face. I wondered what had happened to him, to me, wondered if he still thought he knew what death looked like. I wanted to probe him, talk about all the things neither of us had said. Then, whatever it was, vanished. Or maybe it never existed. He bobbed his head in a goodbye. I tossed him a little parting salute. He marched down the aisle, stepped on the rubber mat, which threw open the door, and was gone.

THE GIRL AT THE AQUARIUM

I had not been to the aquarium in twenty years; then, in a week's time, I had occasion to go twice. The first visit was business. One of my company's clients, a Kuwaiti gentleman, had never seen fish in tanks. Shortly after that, some cousins of my late wife were in town and, perhaps making an unconscious link with Ben Franklin's long-ago quip about fish and relatives, I brought them there. With their children, they took up a stand in front of the huge main tank where the kids watched with hungry eyes, waiting for the sharks to "cream" something. Not feeling quite so sanguine, I strolled among the other exhibits: the penguins and seals and parti-colored tropical fish. That's where I saw the girl in the raincoat, and it came to me that she had been at the aquarium when I had visited a few days before.

Isn't it curious how you can see something, and yet, at the same time, not see it?

For years my wife and I had kept an unvarying morning pattern: into the car with our mugs of coffee for the drive to the commuter rail station. One morning, talking around a luxuriant yawn, Paula pointed to a small tree (I later learned it was a Chinese dogwood) and said wasn't it beautiful. For five days a week, morning and night, four seasons a year, for ten years, I had passed that tree and never seen it. After that, however, and after Paula died, and before I moved to the city to live, that dogwood became my private barometer, an instrument of such subtle and delicate calibration that it marked the march of time. Not simply the seasons, no; gradually, as I learned to read it in my passing, I could see the literal change of each day.

Each long . . . lonely . . . day.

I mention this only to point out how we can see but not see. It wasn't until the second time I noticed the slender young woman at the aquarium that I knew I had seen her there the first time.

She stood by a tall tank of tropical fish, which were swimming (almost flying, it seemed) on their delicate fins. But I paid scarce notice to the fish, concentrating my gaze on her.

Her face, though not beautiful by any current vogue, was a revelation, so clear and soft and striking, and with a hint of something else which I could not name. Her skin was pale, and it shimmered with emerald and aquamarine ribbons of light from the tank. She stood apart from the relentlessly shifting schools of visitors, her wavery red-gold hair spread in a soft fan over her slender shoulders. The lavender raincoat she wore was of a stylish cut (with some splashy designer label on the inside, I could imagine) but tasteful, too, and buttoned demurely to the top.

As I watched from my distance, however, it was her face that I kept coming back to, like a thirsty man to a fountain. It was a fresh, small-featured face, lean, and touched, it came to me then, with a quality of sadness. Then my relatives were dragging me off in quest of new excitements, and with a small lurch of sadness of my own, I went.

* * *

For some reason, I found myself returning to the aquarium on several occasions after that. And each time, I was surprised to find the young woman standing before the same tank of bright, swimming forms. Then I knew that was why I had gone back.

She remained as before: self-contained, betraying no awareness—neither through a look, nor gesture nor expression—that she had seen me or anyone else in the forever changing guard of faces. Her focus seemed always to be on the delicately moving fish in the tank.

As before, she wore the lavender coat, closed at the top with a large purple button. As before, her hair lay soft across her thin shoulders. And again I sensed in her intent regard, a lambent sadness.

Within me there was kindling a low fever.

I visited often; at lunch hour if nothing was pressing; weekends. I felt a kind of self-mocking embarrassment, like a high-schooler watching a dream girl across the safe distance of a study hall. After a time I grew uncomfortable being there, caught, I soon saw, in a worsening spell of indecision. However, rather than act in some way—boldly approach her (a knack I have never mastered), or desist in my visits—I discovered myself scrutinizing her more and more closely, looking, I realized, for some flaw, some human imperfection so unacceptable that I could turn away at last in cowardly relief.

But what fault was there? The pale skin? Her too-slender form for her height? The raincoat worn in all weathers and perhaps, though it may have been light refractions from the tank, starting to show smudges of wear? These couldn't matter. More than anything, I longed for the freshness she bore like a fragrance, longed even to know her sadness.

One Saturday I saw her speak when addressed by an aquarium attendant. He may have made some quiet joke, for she smiled faintly. A bold man perhaps, or one not under the same spell as I, he began a conversation, pointing out, I presumed, the varieties of fish. She was polite (very much so), but not a ready participant in the exchange, and it ended with him touching his hat and moving off. And yet I envied him. He had made, however tenuous, a link.

It's a dismaying sensation to be at middle age, still trapped in the discomfiture one associates with adolescence. Nor am I an especially shy man; reticent, true, but I have done well in business. And yet, each time I saw her, I felt hapless. Rehearsed opening lines, words of repartee, what the popular media, ever ready to offer advice, like to call "icebreakers," fell like worthless coins in my mind, opening no turnstile. And always I would go away before she did, full of self-recrimination at the ways a grown man, a lonely widower, could behave.

One day, as I visited the aquarium during a lunch break, an hour I spent secretly watching her, she left before I did. Oddly this threw me into a panic, for it meant a change, perhaps an opportunity I had not foreseen; and I doubted I was up to it. With damp palms and a quick heart I set off in her wake.

She moved steadily away from the busy downtown area, a place I had long since decided was the ocean that our strange upright species swam in among the sunken mountains of stone and glass. Now I moved there alone, fearful, and yet curiously alive with a sense of unknown purpose.

I trailed her into the north end of the city, amid the narrowing streets of brick warehouses, where the smell of the harbor mingled with the aromas of small cafes and the stinks of trade. As the throngs thinned, I saw her turn a corner. She never looked back.

Hurrying, I rounded the same corner, saw the flicker of her raincoat as she entered a long, shabby building that appeared to be a small factory of some kind. My heart changed tempo twice, going to a surge of relief that there would be no confrontation after all, and then to the dull pound of my real loss. I had missed her.

* * *

I went to the aquarium on two consecutive days that week, and as before she was in her place in front of the tank. But something had changed. Possibly, I told myself, it was my feeling that the thing (I could hardly call it a relationship) must go somewhere or be stopped. I had had my chances. To continue not to act would undermine me. Already my life had lurched off its accustomed tracks. My days now were built around trips to the aquarium. Maybe my work performance had begun to suffer. I felt different. The other thought that came to me, however (and this was more unsettling), was that
she was different, too. And on that second day I knew how.

Slipping nearer to her in a sudden holiday thickening of the crowds, I watched her gazing into the tank. As one vivid and solitary fish finned near on a tracery of indigo wings, she reached to touch the glass, and I saw a shadow track down her cheek.

There was condensation on the tank, which could have been what I saw—a reflection thrown by light on the screen of her pale face—but I knew better.

Desperate by that time, with a nightly ache in my heart and no appetite for old habits, I determined to quit my foolish pursuit. I resolved to stay away from the aquarium.

* * *

I have said that, by nature, I am a creature of discipline and pattern. For more than a dozen years I rode the same train, morning and evening. For two decades I had held fast to the same job. So for one, two, three days I clung to my desk come lunchtime. I let paperwork and the telephone hold me there. On the weekend I rented a car and left the city, drove, for no clear reason, to the suburban town where Paula and I had lived.

In choosing the city after she died, I had chosen illusion. By living among a million people I could believe I had human contact. The reality was I had been a stranger, unaware except in the deepest, most inexpressible way, of how lonely I had grown. Oh, I had acquaintances, and fellow workers, and a neighbor or two I greeted in the apartment building halls, but my time was spent alone. And, in truth, I preferred that, because, having married young and devoted myself to my wife and my work, I had become accustomed to a margin of solitude. I had long ago decided, as I would see the morning faces on the train, or the noontime throngs on the streets, that it was our common destiny to be alone. And while I accepted this, I could no longer pretend to like it.

But I am straying from what I want to say.

That Saturday I went back to my old town, where I visited no one, thinking I was content to ride past our former house, to eat at a restaurant where I neither recognized nor was recognized by a soul. Then I drove the route Paula and I had traveled all those mornings and evenings. I came at length to the dogwood tree, in the froth of its early spring regalia now. I stopped the car and spent long moments just looking, getting caught up on all that had passed.

That Monday I called in to the office sick. After a morning of increasingly restless indecision, I went . . . well, you know where I went.

But she was not there.

In fact, the tank she usually stood before was empty, filled only with air. Experiencing a queasy dismay, I found an attendant, the same man who had conversed with her that time, and quizzed him. He told me that during the night the power had gone out. The aquarium's oxygen and filtration systems had shut down until emergency generators had taken over. Fish in the other tanks had had no problem. "But these tropical species," he explained, his cap crushed in his big hands, "they're so fragile . . . "

It was a day of drizzle, with a saline wind springing off the sea. Randomly at first (I thought), then with purpose (I knew), my steps were taking me away from the busy heart of the city. I found myself hurrying toward the north end where, with unconscious precision, my feet retraced the route they had taken that day when I had followed the girl. Outside the door she had entered I paused, hearing the dull clangor of machines within, trying in vain to peer through smudged glass to know what lay beyond. At last I went in.

The air was hot and full of dust. Long ribbons of belting wobbled from sprockets in the dimness, and the noise was painful. Women in kerchiefs yanked objects off of conveyors. I almost left. Then I noticed several women clustered at a time clock, waiting to punch cards. I approached.

Did they know (I faltered without a name) the young woman with the red-gold hair . . . the lavender raincoat?

Suspicious glances. Who was I? Why'd I want to know? But my intensity must have convinced them. One woman offered a detail. The girl was going to lose her job if she didn't watch out. The boss . . . he was one bastard. A second woman gave a name. Clarice. A third mentioned an address.

The next voice was harsh, booming over the machine sounds. Who the hell are you? What are you doing here? The boss. I fled.

I hurried through narrow, alien streets, asking directions twice. The old brick buildings gave the illusion of rusting in the gray rain, like the moldering hulks of ships that have been long sunk, and more than ever I felt I was underwater, drowned among the relics of a life I had somehow, unknowingly, chosen. With a desperation that frightened me, I knew I had to escape . . . at least to try.

The street was a slum: rundown tenements, sidewalks heaped with trash, which oozed in the rain and stank. A voice at my back menaced: "Move your carcass or I'll move it for you!"

I stepped aside to let a lurching, blind-drunk man paddle past.

I found the number. In the dim hallway I stood before several doors, water from my clothes puddling on the greasy linoleum. Summoning courage I knocked on a door until a moon-faced man in chinos and a stained undershirt appeared. I told him, "Clarice."

He eyed me warily, sucking his teeth. "You a social worker?"

No, I said. It was personal.

A long moment the man studied me, as if deciding something. Then he stepped at me, pulled his door shut behind him. "Look, I'm the super. It's none of my business, and there's folks around who'd give me hell for nosing in—my wife among them—but look . . . if she's your girl, you ought to get her out of here."

I swallowed, my mind swarming with chaotic thoughts.

"It ain't right," he went on. "The way that old uncle and his woman treat her, making her do everything for them like they were invalids and not just lazy slobs. That uncle's mean as a snake, swinging that cane like it was the executioner's ax. He nearly chopped me when I stuck my nose in once and told him I was gonna call the cops if he hit her one more time."

"He hit her?"

"I would've called them too, but the girl, she was so scared she denied he done it. Said she fell down. But I hear them." He sent a glance upward. "Sounds come through the ceiling. She buttons that coat to hide the bruises. So if she's your girl . . . "

I was already scaling the rickety stairs when I heard it: crashing sounds, voices, an old woman's, and then a man's. I stopped and listened, trembling where I stood.

"Where is she? Goddammit! I'll wail her! She's supposed to be here!"

"I need my cigarettes. Where the hell is she?"

For a moment I was rooted, my blood running with a cool plasma of terror. Then I was fleeing, sinking down the stairs, envisioning the delicate fish which floated in their pristine, silent world, seeing her face when she put it near the glass and a tear had run, using these images as I had used the dogwood tree after my wife died . . .

Heartsick and cold, I ran and ran, past where the buildings gave out in a final wretched string, and before I knew it I was at the harbor, only a chain link fence and a weed-grown lot separating me from the water.

Where I saw her.

Again the reactions of surprise and non-surprise. My heart churning. She stood far out on the last rocks of a breakwater, a lone figure, her hair whipped by the wet gusts, coat wrapped tight to her slender body.

She was staring down at the gray sea that lurched on the boulders beneath her. Then her coat bellied suddenly with wind as she began to unbutton it.

In a fever I looked for a way past the fence, but the only gate was far off. The thought came that I could still get away, fly from there, back to my desk, my work, my life. . . .

Panting with the effort I dragged myself to the top of the fence. As I tried to climb down the other side, I lost my grip and fell. Ignoring a sharp lance of pain, I got up.

She let her coat drop away.

I began to run across the unpaved lot.

She stepped to the edge of the rocks.

I yelled.

A single word. All I had breath for.

Stop?

Don't?

Clarice?

I don't know which it was. A sound shouted into the wind, which carried it to her, making her turn and stare with large, frightened eyes.

But I had no breath for anything more. I was splashing across the rain-whipped mud, no longer thinking of the loneliness that was my life, only desperate for something I did not yet know, but which I had to find out, running toward the girl who maybe, instead of bright, delicate fish, was seeing me.

David Daniel grew up on the South Shore of Boston. He has been a college professor, a journalist, a carpenter, a tennis pro, and a "brain slicer" at Harvard Medical School. He was the Jack Kerouac Visiting Writer in Residence at the University of Massachusetts, Lowell, where he also serves as an adjunct instructor. Currently he works at the Lowell Middlesex Academy Charter School, teaching English and phys ed.

DAVID DANIEL ALSO WROTE

The Saga of Meek's Café
Axolotl
The Ostrich
Ark
The Tuesday Man
The Heaven Stone
The Skelly Man
Murder at the Baseball Hall of Fame (with Chris Carpenter)
White Rabbit
Goofy Foot
The Marble Kite
Reunion

65

Six Off 66
stories by **David Daniel**